STRETCHED TOO THIN

SUPER HUMAN

STRETCHED TOO THIN

RAELYN DRAKE

darbycreek
MINNEAPOLIS

Darby Creek
A division of Lerner Publishing Group, Inc.
241 First Avenue North
Minneapolis, MN 55401 USA

For reading levels and more information, look up this title at
www.lernerbooks.com.

The images in this book are used with the permission of: © iStockphoto.com/Vladimirovic; © iStockphoto.com/fotoVoyager; © iStockphoto.com/kirstypargeter; © iStockphoto.com/sinemaslow.

Main body text set in Janson Text LT Std 12/17.5.
Typeface provided by Adobe Systems.

Library of Congress Cataloging-in-Publication Data

Names: Drake, Raelyn, author.
Title: Stretched too thin / Raelyn Drake.
Description: Minneapolis : Darby Creek, [2018] | Series: Superhuman | Summary: Days after he turns sixteen, skateboarder Evan Wu-Kopecky discovers his body's super-stretchiness and immediately decides to become a local superhero, even though his best friend Layla questions whether Stretch Guy is merely looking for an endorsement.
Identifiers: LCCN 2017010747 (print) | LCCN 2017032838 (ebook) | ISBN 9781512498363 (eb pdf) | ISBN 9781512498288 (lb : alk. paper)
Subjects: | CYAC: Superheroes—Fiction. | Skateboarding—Fiction. | Fame—Fiction.
Classification: LCC PZ7.1.D74 (ebook) | LCC PZ7.1.D74 St 2018 (print) | DDC [Fic]—dc23
LC record available at https://lccn.loc.gov/2017010747

Manufactured in the United States of America
1-43579-33360-6/5/2017

To my sister, Aina, who will forever
be a better skater than me, since she's
mastered the art of not falling off
the board.

SIXTEEN YEARS AGO, ON APRIL 12, SIX PEOPLE FROM AROUND THE COUNTRY WERE BORN WITH A HIDDEN SPECIAL ABILITY.

On their sixteenth birthday, they each develop their special ability for the first time. Whether they can soar through the clouds, run faster than the speed of light, or tear through a brick wall, all the teenagers must choose how to use their powers. Will they keep their abilities secret? Will they use them only to benefit themselves? Or will they attempt to help others—even if the risks are greater than they could imagine? One way or another, each teen will have to learn what it means to be . . . superhuman.

1

The banner over the Greenfair Gardens skate park gates flapped in the cool spring breeze: SICK TRICK TEEN SKATE SEMIFINALS—FRIDAY, APRIL 22. Evan avoided looking at it as he rolled his skateboard back and forth with one foot. The memory of not qualifying for the semifinals still stung. Late in the evening on a Tuesday the park was empty except for him and Layla, who stood a couple of feet away fiddling with settings on her video camera.

Layla sighed loudly. "Hey, birthday boy, are you going to try the trick again or not?"

Evan massaged his shoulder. It still ached from where he had hit the ground when he lost his board on the last attempt. "Don't rush me."

"Dude, c'mon, it's getting late and traffic is always a mess at the freeway interchange. The one with the driver's license gets to make the rules." She stuck her tongue out at Evan. "The one with the learner's permit is lucky I don't make him take the city bus when he wants to go to the fancy skate park across town."

Layla and Evan usually skated at Centennial Skate Plaza, which was only a couple of blocks from their houses. But the skate park at Greenfair Gardens was newer, bigger, and much less run-down. It even had benches, which Layla took advantage of now, plopping down next to her camera bag and stifling a yawn.

"Why don't you just go back to doing 180 ollies?" Layla suggested. "You're good at those, and you could throw in kickflips to make it look cooler. Unless you start landing some clean tricks, you're going to have a very short Sponsor Me video."

Evan eyed the flat cement strip that stretched between two raised sections, trying to visualize himself getting the trick right and reminding himself to brake before he got to the sloping part. "No one is gonna want to sponsor me if I can't stick a complicated trick like a 360 ollie. I need to kick my board up and spin *all* the way around in the air before I land. Halfway isn't going to cut it if I want a skateboarding sponsorship and free gear. Think of all the publicity!"

"Think of the dinner we could be eating right now!" Layla snapped back teasingly. "My parents said they invited your dad and brother to our house to celebrate your birthday."

Evan could almost hear his stomach growl. "Tell them not to let my brother eat it all before we get there! Isaac looks cute and innocent, but for a ten-year-old, he can put food away like a quarterback."

Layla laughed. "All right, how about you give it one more go?"

Evan took a deep breath. He stood with one foot on his board and pushed off, gliding over the smooth concrete. He bent his knees, shifted his weight, and popped the board, kicking the tail end down and rotating his shoulders in preparation for the three-hundred-and-sixty-degree spin.

He spun in a circle once, twice . . . and then he kept spinning and spinning. His stomach churned as the park hurtled by in a dizzying blur. He landed hard and, remembering to bend his knees at the last second, miraculously managed to stay on his board, continuing in the same direction he had been going.

With a celebratory whoop, he dragged his back foot on the ground to skid to a stop. He couldn't tell if the prickling sensation that crawled up his back was from goose bumps or the thrill of success. He turned to give the camera an exhilarated thumbs-up, but his grin faded when he saw Layla's expression.

"Why do you look so freaked out? That was awesome! Forget 360, I think I spun around twice! Only pro skaters can manage a 720 ollie!"

Layla's eyes were wide. She held up her video camera. "I think you'd better come see this."

Evan grabbed his skateboard and walked over to her. He took off his helmet and ran a hand through his dark hair, enjoying the cool breeze after he'd worked up a bit of a sweat.

Evan watched the video. Everything seemed normal: he had skated forward, started to twist in preparation for the ollie, and then—

His brain refused to make sense of what it was seeing. He blinked rapidly. "Can I see that again?"

Layla restarted the video and turned on slow motion playback.

Evan watched as his entire body seemed to corkscrew, twisting tighter and tighter like a coiled spring, and then unwinding in an explosive burst.

"Seven full revolutions." He multiplied it out in his head. "A 2520 ollie." *But that's not physically possible*, he thought.

Layla was still staring at him, chewing on her lower lip. "You should probably have my mom look at you. What if it's broken?"

"What if *what* is broken?"

Layla flushed. "Your spine? I don't know. There's got to be something wrong."

"The last thing I want is Dr. Hakim telling my dad I injured myself skateboarding. Again." Evan felt along his spine. "It doesn't hurt or anything—"

Layla yelped in surprise, taking a quick step backward.

Evan followed her eyes. The arm he had reached behind himself had kept extending, and his hand appeared over his shoulder.

"Awesome!" Evan exclaimed. He gave Layla a small wave.

Layla wrinkled her nose. "Then how do you explain . . . *that*?"

Evan shrugged. He wondered if he could do it on command. He looked around him, but the park was deserted this close to dusk on a Tuesday night. He closed his eyes. If he concentrated, he could feel the same strange feeling that had run down his back creeping along his legs. It was almost a dull ache—like growing pains but pleasant. *It feels good, actually,* he thought. He attempted to extend his legs.

He heard Layla gasp and opened his eyes. His head was now a full foot above Layla's.

"Whoa," Evan said. "I've always wanted to be taller than you."

"That's not normal," Layla said as she stared up at him.

"Layla, do you realize what this means?" Evan asked her, barely able to contain his excitement.

Layla arched an eyebrow. "What?"

"I have . . ." Evan paused for dramatic effect, "*superpowers!*"

Layla gave a strangled laugh. "That's the conclusion you're drawing from all of this?"

Evan contracted his legs so he shrank back down to normal height. "What else could it be?"

"Some sort of weird disease that changes all your bones to rubber?" Layla shook her head in disbelief. "Wow," she muttered, "superpowers almost sound more believable."

"See?" Evan said. He put his helmet back on and hopped on his board. Before Layla could protest, he set off across the park. He landed a few aerial tricks on the quarter pipe ramp with ease. It was like his entire body was made of elastic.

"This is great!" he shouted as he skated back. "I would totally crush the competition in the Teen Skate Semifinals. That would show those stupid judges from Sick Trick Industries for not letting me compete!"

He wasn't looking at Layla, but he could imagine her eye roll from her tone of voice. "Evan, you need to get over that. So you didn't qualify for the next round, no big deal."

Evan stopped short. "No big deal? What if there are reps from major skateboard companies or brands scouting for talent?"

"There aren't going to be any good reps there. Trust me, the Internet is going to be your ticket to fame. We'll upload your Sponsor Me video . . . I mean, I guess we can edit out the bit with the—the—you know."

"Superpowers?" Evan prompted with an excited grin.

"I was going to say 'crazy mutant abilities.'"

"That makes it sound like you think I'll get

taken away for scientific testing. Like Area 51, government agents stuff."

Layla shrugged. "I'm still not convinced that you aren't sick. Were you bitten by any radioactive bugs? Struck by lightning? Born during an eclipse?"

Evan's eyes widened. "Layla, you're a genius!"

Layla frowned. "I don't know what you're thinking, but I can tell I'm not going to like it."

"What's the point of having superpowers if I don't use my gift to make the world a better place? I'll become a superhero!" He struck a heroic pose with his hands on his hips, although the effect was ruined when Layla snorted.

"A superhero? Really?"

"Have you got a better idea? This opportunity is too cool to waste. Think of all the crime I could prevent!"

"With stretch powers?"

"Sure!"

"I mean I guess you could reach up into trees to rescue stuck cats or . . . kites." Layla's phone beeped and she read the text. "My dad says dinner will be ready soon. He made baklava for dessert just because he knows it's your favorite."

"Fine, let's go. I'm starving."

Layla put away her video camera, and they headed to where her yellow jeep was parked. "Not a word about this to my parents, okay? You know my mom will freak out and make you come to the hospital so she can run a bunch of tests on you."

Evan held up his hands. "No worries."

"Can you control your"—she made air quotes—"powers?"

Evan realized he wasn't sure. "So far I've had to concentrate to be able to activate it. We should be safe."

He crossed his fingers. Or at least he tried, but they twisted around each other and tied themselves into a bow.

Layla's eyebrows raised as she stared at his fingers. "Great."

2

The next day after dinner, Evan and Layla met
at the closer skate park, Centennial Skate Plaza.
"Skate park" was a loose term in this case.
All the neighborhood had been able to afford
were a couple of pre-built metal obstacles
that sat rusting on the pitted surface of the
old tennis court. The original flat bar rail
had disappeared years ago, leaving only some
protruding bolts that had once secured it to the
ground. Luckily there was a set of stairs with a
handrail set into the side of the grassy hill.

   Evan secretly liked how run-down
Centennial was. It kept away all the newbie
skaters and posers, meaning that he and

Layla usually had the place to themselves. Of course, their parents weren't thrilled about the safety hazards of the deteriorating equipment, but Evan and Layla suspected they were mostly happy that their children were doing something constructive with their free time.

Evan was pleasantly surprised that Layla had agreed to hang out two days in a row. Lately, it seemed, she had been way too busy with her films. She was hoping to get a filmmaker scholarship to her dream college, and she was always stuck in front of her computer editing projects. Well, "stuck" was the term Evan would use. Layla seemed to enjoy the hours fussing over her films frame by frame. Evan would much rather be skating.

The day had been warm and sunny, but as dusk crept in it grew chilly. As usual they had the skate park to themselves.

Layla took her camera out of her bag and fiddled with the settings. "You're still set on this superhero thing?" she asked. She seemed resigned; years of friendship had prepared her for Evan's grand schemes.

"Obviously!" Evan said. "I've already got a costume worked out and everything."

"A costume? Really?" Layla put a hand to her mouth to cover a smirk. "Oh, please tell me you didn't go out and buy some sort of brightly colored spandex ensemble?"

It was Evan's turn to roll his eyes. "Of course not. Why would I want to draw attention to myself? I'm wearing my costume right now." He gestured to his outfit. He had settled on a pair of black runner's leggings and his favorite black skateboard hoodie.

"And now for the cool bit!" he said. He had borrowed his dad's jogging mask. It was designed to protect the lower half of the face on cold-weather runs, so his dad probably wouldn't miss it until next winter. Evan pulled up the mask now. With the hood of his sweatshirt up, only his eyes were visible.

Layla laughed. "You look like a dorky ninja. Why didn't you get a mask that covered your entire face? I can still tell it's you."

"That's only because you know me so well. When I'm running around town fighting injustice at night, no one will be able to get a good look at me. Besides, a full-face ski mask looks way too 'evil henchman.'"

"Whoa, whoa, wait, go back," Layla said, putting up one hand. "Did you seriously say 'fighting injustice'?"

"Yeah," Evan said. "What do you think superheroes do?"

"I know this isn't the swankiest neighborhood, but it's not exactly some seedy underbelly of the town either. Where are you going to find injustice to fight?"

Evan shrugged. "It doesn't have to be major crime, but stuff still happens around town. If I wait long enough there's bound to be something. In the meantime, we can talk about what my awesome superhero name will be."

"Mr. Slamtastic."

"I feel like you're not taking this seriously."

"Stretch Guy?"

"I was hoping for something a little cooler and more mysterious."

"Why do you even need a secret identity?" Layla asked.

"To protect my friends and family, obviously," Evan said. "You should know that—you've read more comic books than I have."

"Yeah, but those guys have powerful archenemies. You haven't beaten any criminals yet, let alone attracted the attention of a dangerous super villain."

"Okay, then I just need a name because it's cool. C'mon, how many people have a chance to be superheroes? How many people can do this?" He turned his head like an owl so that he could look behind him.

Layla sighed. "Okay, so it wasn't a dream."

"Nope! Definitely not a dream," Evan said proudly. "I spent all last night after dinner practicing, just to make sure I can control it."

"So what am I supposed to do while you're fighting injustice?" Layla asked. "Or is it my job to come bail you out when you get in trouble?"

"No, you get to help! You're going to be my sidekick."

Layla raised an eyebrow and Evan immediately wished he had thought of a better way to phrase that.

She crossed her arms. "And what exactly does that involve?"

"Umm, I was thinking you could film me being a hero, so there's proof. Like a Sponsor Me video but with superpowers. And then post the footage to a website. And design the website, I guess. And I probably need you to drive me around. And—"

Layla laughed. "So I'm your camerawoman, biographer, techie, and chauffeur?"

Evan felt his face grow hot. "I mean, yeah, you're obviously an important part of the whole operation."

"I'm basically your manager, then."

"That's exactly the word I was looking for."

"I bet it was."

"And I figured you could use it as filmmaking practice."

Layla sighed. "I'll do it for you as a friend. But how am I supposed to hide my identity?"

"I figured you could keep a low profile," he looked at the brightly colored scarf on her head, "and maybe switch to some darker clothes."

Layla snorted. "Should I hide in the bushes like superhero paparazzi?"

Evan laughed. "Let's find some injustice first, and then we can work out the details."

They both scanned the park. A couple of cars passed by, a group of middle schoolers riding their bikes, a woman walking her dog. Nothing out of the ordinary for this time of evening. No sign that anyone needed a superhero to save the day.

"Are we seriously going to sit here in the dark and wait for injustice to happen?" Layla asked, wrapping her jacket around her. "It's getting cold. Can we at least skate for a while first?"

Evan checked his phone, reluctant to give up on his very first night of superhero-ing. "Maybe there's something going on somewhere else. Do you know how to access police alerts?"

Layla pulled out her own phone. "Those are only posted after the fact when the officer files the report, so that's not really helpful— you need a crime that's happening right now." She scrolled through her social media newsfeed. "Here we go! Someone posted that there are a bunch of cop cars at the gas station over on Seventy-Second and Lake. That's all the way across town though. I don't know if we'll get there in time—"

Evan was already on his board and heading down the street. He thought he heard Layla yell something about taking her car, but Evan wanted to test out a theory he had come up with the night before. He didn't want to have to rely on Layla to drive him around if he was going to be a masked crusader. Her yellow jeep would be far too recognizable. That left just his skateboard as a mode of transport. A skateboard would never be fast enough—under normal circumstances.

He stretched his arms out in front of him, gripping the pavement to propel himself forward. *Turbo-skating*, he thought, smiling as the wind rushed past him.

The sun had gone down and he hoped it was dark enough that no one would notice him. Just to be on the safe side, he stuck to the residential streets without bright streetlights.

Dragging his back foot on the ground to brake, Evan slowed down as he approached the gas station.

"Here we go," he said under his breath.

3

The police had already blocked off the area with caution tape. Glass from the smashed gas station window littered the parking lot, glinting in the flashing lights from the cop cars. There were three cars out front, but Evan couldn't see any police officers. He wondered if they were inside talking to the store owner. He tried to see if there was anyone in the back of the cop cars, but the tinted windows made it impossible to tell. It looked like there had been a robbery. Evan paused, unsure what a superhero was supposed to do in a situation like this.

Bystanders huddled in a small group on the sidewalk across the street. Evan wondered if they lived in the houses nearby and had heard the commotion, or if they had been in the gas station when the robbery happened. He suddenly realized that they were staring at him, leaning in close to whisper to one another. One bystander looked toward the gas station, as though considering whether to go inform the cops. Evan realized that it looked a little suspicious to be lurking near the scene of a recent crime wearing dark clothes and a mask that obscured half his face.

Evan cleared his throat quietly and got back on his skateboard. He skated down the street away from the gas station as casually as he could. He ducked into an alleyway that he knew was a shortcut to a road that looped back to Centennial Skate Plaza.

He didn't hear any signs that he was being followed, and Evan had just started to relax when he collided with someone. Evan's board went flying, but he stretched out one arm and caught it neatly and stretched out his other arm to catch himself before he hit the ground. He pushed himself back up to a standing position. The whole thing had taken less than a second.

Evan froze when he realized who he had hit. The older man lying on his back with the wind knocked out of him was Mr. Mendez, a math teacher from his school. Evan had been in his class for ninth grade algebra. The shortcut, Evan knew, wasn't exactly secret, and if Mr. Mendez lived in this area . . . Evan desperately hoped the alleyway was dark enough that Mr. Mendez wouldn't recognize him.

"I'm so—" Evan was going to say *sorry*, but Mr. Mendez held up his hands.

"Take what you want and go," he said. "I'm only a teacher. There's nothing in my briefcase but math quizzes. There's a little cash in my wallet if you need it. Just don't take my wedding ring."

Horrified that his old teacher thought he was mugging him, Evan tried to explain. "I'm not—" He hesitated. What if Mr. Mendez recognized his voice? This secret identity stuff was harder than he thought.

"Sorry," Evan said in as gruff and raspy a voice as he could manage. He stretched out his arms and pulled Mr. Mendez to his feet, then turned and ran.

He could hear Mr. Mendez shouting for the police. Not that Evan could blame his teacher if he thought he had just been mugged. Evan turned and stretched his arms up to the roof of the building next to him, throwing his skateboard up, then grabbing onto the fire escape ladder. It was harder to pull himself up than he thought it would be. He might be able to stretch, but he didn't have super strength, and he had always had trouble climbing the rock wall in P.E. But Evan found that if he stopped trying to lift, and instead focused on de-stretching his arms, he could reel himself up. He heaved himself over the lip of the building and crouched on top of it for a moment, trying to catch his breath.

He thought he could hear police sirens in the distance. He scurried across the roof. There was a gap between buildings, but he could extend his legs and step across.

Evan reached the end of the block of shops. If he wanted to stay off the ground, he would have to step from house to house. But these roofs sloped, and besides, someone was sure to hear him.

He was dangling from the edge of the roof, trying to lower himself down, when his hand slipped. Too surprised to scream, Evan instead landed on the ground with an *ooph*. He stood up and brushed himself off. He felt fine, even though he had fallen at least thirty feet. And was it just his imagination, or had he *bounced* when he hit the ground . . . ?

Headlights cut through the darkness behind him. Evan was about to panic when a yellow jeep pulled up next to him.

"Get in, dummy," Layla hissed.

On the way home, Evan explained to Layla what had happened. Now that the danger was over, Evan could feel the excitement building again. He might not have accomplished much in the crime-fighting department, but he had done things that would have been impossible without his new powers.

"You know, I was joking about bailing you out, Evan," Layla said. "I can't believe you tackled Mr. Mendez."

"I didn't tackle him, I bumped into him!" Evan protested.

"You're lucky you didn't give the poor man a heart attack." She shook her head. "I don't know why you couldn't wait for me to drive you instead of taking off like that." They had pulled into the Hakims' driveway, separated by a thin strip of grass from the Wu-Kopeckys' driveway.

Layla frowned and looked more closely at his hands. "I thought you said you were propelling yourself down the road and scaling buildings?"

Evan looked down at his hands. "Yeah?"

"Then why aren't your hands and feet cut up? You should at least have skinned them. We've both fallen enough while skateboarding to know that."

She's right, Evan thought. He hadn't even considered it in all the excitement. But the skin on his hands and feet was unbroken. It wasn't even red.

"I—I don't know." Evan wondered if maybe he *should* let Layla's mother look at him. Dr. Hakim might be able to figure out what was going on with him.

"Well, it wasn't the most successful first day of being a superhero," Layla said. "Are you sure you still want to do this?"

Evan nodded. "I'll get better at it. I just need practice."

Layla sighed and gave him a small smile. "I'll charge my camera, then."

4

"Your website is ready to go," Layla announced the next day as she sat down next to Evan at their usual lunch table.

"You're the best!" Evan said in between mouthfuls of pizza.

Layla shrugged. "I just used one of the premade templates, so it's nothing special. I uploaded the ollie video from your birthday. Don't worry," she said as Evan's head jerked up. "I blurred out your face so no one can tell it's you."

Evan chewed thoughtfully on a french fry. "We'll need more video footage."

"I could have gotten some great footage last

night if you hadn't run off without me," Layla muttered.

"Yeah, yeah, I know," Evan said. He glanced around to make sure no one was looking, and then stretched his hand across the table to snag the pudding cup off Layla's tray.

She wrinkled her nose at him and stole one of his french fries. "So," she said, pointing at him with the fry, "have you given any more thought to why all this is happening?"

Evan shrugged. "Does it matter?"

"People don't just wake up one day with *superpowers*," Layla said, mouthing the last word before continuing at a normal volume. "Something must have caused this."

"I guess the first time I noticed anything weird was on Tuesday," Evan said.

"You mean your birthday?" Layla's eyes widened. "Your *sixteenth* birthday."

Evan paused with a spoonful of pudding halfway to his mouth. "What's so special about turning sixteen? Besides finally being able to take my driving test so you don't have to give me rides everywhere."

Layla scoffed. "It's an important birthday in *so* many fantasy novels! Characters are always discovering secret abilities when they turn sixteen. They usually end up being some sort of 'Chosen One' and have some grand destiny to fulfill."

"Really?" Evan said, grinning. "I should read fantasy more often."

Layla narrowed her eyes. "Don't let it go to your head. Unless we all missed the mysterious prophecy foretelling your birth, I don't think you're a Chosen One."

"What else is special about April twelfth?" Evan mused.

"Start of the Civil War?" Layla suggested. "I think that whole thing with Fort Sumter went down on April twelfth."

"Someone's been paying attention in history," Evan said with a teasing grin.

"Oh, sure," Layla said as she rolled her eyes. "Make fun of me for being smart and knowing things. Okay then, what do *you* know about April twelfth?"

"Hmm." Evan pulled his phone out of his

pocket and searched the date. "April twelfth was also the day that Russian cosmonaut guy—Yuri Gagarin—became the first human in space," he said. "So it could be aliens?"

Layla nearly choked on the last of her milk as they both started laughing.

They were interrupted by the bell signaling the end of lunch.

"Well," Layla said as they cleared their trays, "whatever the reason is, I'm glad you're using your stretch powers for good instead of evil."

***

The next period, during chemistry, the notification light on Evan's phone blinked. He waited to check it until the teacher turned around to write an equation on the board.

You have study hall next hour right? Layla's text read.

Evan checked to make sure the teacher was still distracted and texted back: *yeah why?*

Meet me in gym for hero op!!!

5

When Evan got to the gym, he was surprised to find all of the lights were off.

"Layla?" His whisper echoed in the empty space.

"Over here!"

As his eyes adjusted to the dim light, Evan saw Layla over by the bleachers. Usually the bleachers were retracted against the wall to make room for P.E. classes.

"They're cleaning the bleachers," Layla explained before he could ask. "That's why no one's in here today."

"What's the hero opportunity?" Evan asked.

He heard a strange sound from behind the bleachers. "Was that a meow?"

"The guy who sits behind me in US History said he thought he heard a cat in the gym when student council was hanging up banners earlier today. No one could find it, but I figured out it's stuck behind the bleachers."

"What's a cat doing in the gym in the first place?" Evan asked.

Layla shrugged. "It's like when you see a bird stuck inside the airport. I think the poor thing's a stray."

"And what do you want me to do?"

"Save it, of course," Layla said. "You can stretch and reach it without having to crawl all the way."

Evan frowned. "You don't have your camera."

Layla crossed her arms. "This isn't a publicity stunt. I honestly thought you would be the best person to help this cat."

Evan sighed. "Fine, I'll get it out," he grumbled as he went to the gap between the back of the bleachers and the wall.

"Think of it as superhero extra credit," Layla called.

Evan peered into the shadowy space under the bleachers. "I don't see the stupid cat," he muttered. "Here, kitty, kitty!" he said in a high-pitched voice.

He heard another meow as he ducked under a metal support bar. He had to crouch to walk under the bleachers.

"Careful!" Layla warned.

"It's fine, I think I can see the cat now." Evan could just make out the small orange shape cowering in the dark. "I'm not even sure it's stuck. I think it's just hiding."

"Try to get it out anyway," Layla pleaded. "It's not safe back there. If it's a stray, we can take it to an animal rescue."

Evan stretched his arm out toward the cat, weaving his extended limb over and under the metal bars. "Good kitty," he whispered. It was stuffy behind the bleachers, and he could already feel the sweat beading on his forehead.

His hand was almost close enough to grab the cat when a loud, metallic clunk made Evan jump. The cat hissed and darted past him toward the opening at the end of the bleachers.

"You did it!" Layla shouted. "The cat—"

The loud whine of machinery filled the air.

"Evan, get out of there!"

For a split second Evan was frozen with panic as he realized that the bleachers were closing, sliding back against the wall—step by step, section by section, starting with the far end. Of course, as the bleachers closed, the crawl space behind them disappeared.

The thought of being crushed spurred Evan into action. He scrambled back the way he had come, trying to retract his outstretched arms, but his sweatshirt sleeve kept catching on protruding bolts.

The last section of bleachers shuddered toward the wall with a rumbling like thunder. Evan had almost reached the end as the bleachers closed on him. He tried to make his body as flat as possible, slipping out from behind the bleachers just as they snapped shut.

The P.E. teacher and a custodian stepped into the gym, distracted by whatever they were talking about. Evan and Layla quickly slipped out a side door into an empty hallway before the adults spotted them.

Evan collapsed to the ground, back to his normal dimensions. He felt like a cartoon character that had been smooshed flat and re-inflated like a balloon.

Panting to catch his breath, he looked up at Layla, who was half-sobbing in worry, half-laughing in disbelief. "That was *insane*."

"I wish we could've gotten that on film," Evan moaned, sitting up.

"Malfunctioning bleachers aside, you managed to save a life."

The cat came over and rubbed against Evan's leg. "You know, I'm really more of a dog person."

6

That Saturday, Evan woke up early and checked the superhero website Layla had designed for him. Evan's main concern was the counter that told him how many people had visited the site and watched Stretch Guy videos. *I really need to come up with a cooler superhero name*, Evan thought.

The counter had climbed to 50. Fifty people! It wasn't much in terms of internet fame, but he figured that was more people than who paid attention to him at school. And it was up five people from last night.

Evan scrolled through the videos. He still hadn't been very successful at finding injustice to fight, but Layla was a wizard at editing footage and skater music together to make him look cooler than he was. Evan wished he didn't have to have a secret identity. He would love to have the people at school see these videos and know that it was him. But he thought again about medical tests (he already hated getting shots), and he thought about having to explain all this to his dad and brother, and he realized it was for the best. Besides, Stretch Guy was too cool to worry about everyday problems like upcoming English papers and a B- on a chemistry test. Those were problems for Evan Wu-Kopecky. Stretch Guy had more important things to do.

People had already started commenting on the videos Layla had posted. Some were impressed, some said it was all faked. Evan was a little disappointed that no one seemed to notice how good Layla's camerawork and film editing was.

Evan went downstairs for breakfast. His dad and Isaac were already awake, eating cereal.

"Ah, I thought I had another son around here somewhere," his dad said. "I guess he just overslept again."

"Teens need more sleep," Evan protested as he poured himself a glass of orange juice. "It's a scientific fact." He put bread in the toaster.

"That's why it's better being ten," Isaac said. "We're tougher."

"Oh yeah?" Evan asked, wrapping his arms around Isaac and mussing his hair.

Isaac giggled. "Plus I don't have as much homework!"

Evan rolled his eyes. "Thanks for reminding me."

"Speaking of," their dad said, "how's that English paper coming along? You said you have one due soon, right?"

"I deny everything!" Evan said, spreading peanut butter on his toast.

"I could always ask Layla," his dad said, smirking. "She keeps better track of your homework than you do."

"Argh, fine, I'm working on it," Evan said as though he was being tortured for information. "I promise I'll finish it soon." He sat down across the table from Isaac.

"Try to have it done by next weekend," suggested his dad. "That way you won't be busy when your mom and Darryl fly in to visit for your birthday."

What his dad didn't mention was that his mom and her boyfriend, Darryl, had planned the trip when Evan had assured his mom they could watch him compete in the Sick Trick Teen Skate Semifinals.

He was sure his dad had broken the bad news to her already, but the memory of not qualifying threatened to cloud Evan's good mood.

While their dad went back to reading the newspaper, Evan used one hand to eat his peanut butter toast and stretched the other arm under the table and behind Isaac. After making sure his dad still wasn't paying attention, Evan used his outstretched arm to tap Isaac on the shoulder.

Isaac jumped and spun to look behind him, but Evan had already retracted his arm. Isaac glared suspiciously at Evan, and Evan returned his look with exaggerated innocence.

"What's up?" he asked Isaac, holding up his hands. It took all his effort to maintain a straight face.

"Nothing," Isaac said and flicked a piece of cereal at Evan when their dad wasn't looking.

After loading the breakfast dishes in the dishwasher and again promising his dad that he would work on his English paper, Evan headed for the garage. His dad's car took up half of the space, but the rest was used for storage. There was enough room for Evan to practice tricks like kickflips in private. He wished that he could practice at the skate park during the day, but even Centennial Skate Plaza would be packed on a sunny spring day like this.

Evan spotted something on a shelf that he thought might be just the thing to help him perfect his stretch powers.

Half an hour later, the back door to the garage creaked open. Evan—in the middle of right-hand-green, left-hand-blue, right-foot-red, and left-foot-yellow—shouted and fell over in his hurry to retract his stretchy limbs. He ended up in a tangle of legs and arms on the plastic game-mat.

Layla doubled over laughing when she saw him. "Don't worry, Mr. Superhero. It's just me." She helped Evan to his feet.

After they had finished their English papers and—at Layla's insistence—studied for the next chemistry quiz and Layla had stayed over for dinner—at his dad's insistence—Evan put on his Stretch Guy "costume" and headed for Centennial with Layla.

"If you need the cover of darkness to fight crime," Layla said as they walked, "what are you going to do when the days keep getting longer? The sun sets late enough as it is in April; by summer we'll have to wait until, like, nine o'clock. And you know my parents won't be cool with me leaving the house that late at night. Besides, what if injustice happens during the day?"

Evan shrugged. "I'll figure it out, I guess."

She nodded. "Oh, hey," she started, pulling a small video camera from her bag, "look what I got to capture—more footage of your 'heroics.'" They stopped walking and she attached it to his helmet. "This way I can get some action shots from your perspective."

When they arrived at Centennial, Layla filmed Evan as he tried out new tricks. Everything seemed easier now with his stretch powers. It wasn't just the actual stretching—all his movements were more fluid, the impact as the skateboard wheels hit the cement was less jarring. In comparison, his body before had been stiff and uncoordinated. This new type of skating was exhilarating—a pure adrenaline high.

"What are you going to do with all that footage anyway?" Evan asked Layla as he took a break to catch his breath.

He couldn't really tell in the yellow light from the streetlamp, but he would have sworn that Layla blushed. "I thought I might make a documentary. Like a full-length biopic kind of thing."

"Wow, really?" Evan asked. "Cool! We'll be famous!"

Evan and Layla took a long, roundabout way home from the park, scanning for anything going on. They were passing by the bistro on Whitaker Street when they saw a girl from their school pounding her fist on the door of the darkened restaurant. The rest of the street was deserted.

"Go hide somewhere," Evan whispered to Layla. "It's Sophie, from school. I worked with her last summer when I was a busboy here."

"Now is not the time to flirt!" Layla grumbled under her breath.

"No, I think she needs help."

Layla rolled her eyes but pulled back farther into the shadows as Evan crossed the street.

Evan readjusted his mask to make sure it covered enough of his face. Wanting to avoid a repeat of his embarrassing encounter with Mr. Mendez, Evan cleared his throat loudly to make sure Sophie didn't think he was trying to sneak up on her. She spun around, but her look of alarm quickly turned to one of pleasant surprise.

"Hey," she said, tucking her hair behind her ear, "aren't you that Stretch Guy that everyone is talking about at school?"

Pride swelled in Evan's chest. "People are talking about me at school?" He coughed and lowered his voice. "I mean, yes, I'm Stretch Guy." *So much for coming up with a cooler name.*

"Man, am I glad you're here!" Sophie said. "I accidentally left my purse at work after my shift. I was hoping someone would still be here, but I think they already finished closing and went home." She peered through the dark window, using her hands to shield her eyes. "Now my purse is locked in there until they open for breakfast Monday morning."

Evan wasn't sure what he—what Stretch Guy—was supposed to do to help her. "Can't you call your manager and get them to unlock it for you?"

"I'm too embarrassed," admitted Sophie. She bit her lip. "This is the second time this has happened," she mumbled.

Evan suddenly had an idea. "Don't worry," he assured her, "I've got this."

Encouraged by Sophie's grateful smile, Evan stretched his arm down to the bottom of the door. He furrowed his brow in concentration and flattened his hand until he could slip it under the door. He still hadn't gotten used to the strange feeling of his bones spreading and rearranging under his expanding skin.

Sophie gasped. "Some of the kids at my school are convinced that Stretch Guy is just a hoax," she explained.

Evan didn't answer, trying to focus on his task. He felt around blindly for the door knob and lock. Finally, the lock turned with a satisfying clunk. He pushed the door open with his other hand as he retracted his stretched arm.

Sophie ran inside. Evan could see her shadow as she emerged from behind the counter with her purse and hurried back to the door.

She threw her arms around him. "Thank you so much, Stretch Guy! I owe you big time." She let him out of the hug with a self-conscious chuckle.

"No problem," Evan stammered, waving at Sophie as she rode away on her bike.

Evan was still staring after her when Layla approached a second later. "I hope you enjoyed that, Romeo—"

They jumped as the bistro's security alarm blared.

"She couldn't be bothered to turn off the alarm?" Layla said with a frustrated huff.

"She was worried about her purse—"

"Sure." Layla rolled her eyes and hopped on her skateboard. "Let's get out of here!"

7

"I'm so screwed if they saw my face on a security camera!" Layla said as they walked into her room.

Evan shook his head. "The security alarm system is real, but there aren't any cameras."

"Wait," Layla said, rounding on him. "You *knew* about the alarm system and you still thought it was a good idea to break into the restaurant?"

Evan felt his face grow hot. "I erm—forgot."

Layla wrinkled her nose at him. "You mean you got distracted because you had to show off for Sophie."

She plucked the camera off Evan's helmet and plugged it into her computer. "At least the helmet-cam got some great footage. I was too busy trying not to be seen." She smirked. "Of course, I'll have to edit out some of the shots that linger a bit too long on Sophie."

Evan ignored her. "Well, except for the alarm going off, I think that all went a lot better than when I tried to save the cat."

"I still think you're a long way from striking fear into the hearts of criminals," Layla said, "but you did manage to help someone. Now go downstairs and see if my dad bought any snack food. I've got a whole lot of editing to do, and you still have chemistry homework."

"Right away, Ms. Manager, ma'am," Evan said, dodging her playful punch on his way out of the room.

***

By Monday morning, the visitor counter on the website had jumped to 248. Between Sophie's story and the new video posted on the site, everyone at school was talking about Stretch Guy. Some people still thought he was a fake.

Sophie was popular, though, and all but the most cynical skeptics were swayed by the argument that "Sophie *saw* him do the stretch thing so you *know* it must be true."

Mrs. Kowalski, the physics teacher, was overheard trying to explain how it was physically impossible for anyone to have those sorts of powers, but people mostly ignored her.

After lunch, Layla stopped by Evan's locker so they could walk to class together.

"Isn't this exciting?" Evan said as he grabbed his textbook for US History.

"I guess," Layla said. "If gossip is your thing. My personal philosophy is that no news is good news." She looked around to make sure no one was listening. "It's not like anyone knows it's you. You can't take credit for any of the things they think Stretch Guy has done."

"But *I* know they're talking about me," Evan said. "And hey, what do you mean 'what they *think* Stretch Guy has done'?"

Layla sighed. "Evan, your powers or whatever they are—they're cool, there's no denying that. I'd even go so far as to call them amazing. But it's the sort of thing you show off at parties. It's not really superhero stuff. It's not like you have super strength or super speed. You're just . . . stretchy."

Evan closed his locker harder than he meant to.

"Hey, look, I'm sorry," Layla said.

Evan thought he had been keeping his face neutral, but Layla knew him too well.

"I didn't mean that you're not capable of doing useful things with your powers," she continued. "I just think you haven't found what that *is* yet. You're coasting on fame you haven't really earned."

"I'm trying," Evan said.

Layla smiled. "I know, but hey, what kind of manager would I be if I didn't push you?"

"You're my sidekick."

Layla patted him on the back. "No, I'm not."

Evan laughed. "No. You're not."

***

By Thursday morning, a little more than a week after Evan's sixteenth birthday, the counter was up to 324 and fans were demanding a new video. Some of the comments made it clear that people were tired of seeing the same old thing. They wanted to see what Stretch Guy was *really* capable of.

That was how Evan found himself at Centennial after dinner, standing at the top of the stairs and eyeing the rusty handrail. There were two flights of stairs and a break in the railing between the two. Evan's plan was to do a grind down the first railing, stretch his arms forward to do a handstand on the second railing, then arch his back to plant his feet at the bottom of the steps, followed by the rest of him, and then skate away. Maybe throw in a kickflip at the end for good measure.

He had done rail grinds on a flat bar before, but this was his first time trying it on these stairs. Steeply angled and an extra twenty inches above the ground. *No big deal, right?* He assumed—he hoped—that his stretch powers would make it easy.

Layla had voiced her doubts, but she was in position anyway. She stood on the grassy hill next to the stairs, camera up. "I'm ready when you are, Stretch Guy."

He got a rolling start, then popped up as high as he could to land with his board on the handrail, parallel to the stairs. He slid down the railing on the front and rear axles of his skateboard with the satisfying rasp of metal on metal.

Evan felt the railing wobble, and his stomach gave a sickening lurch as he tipped forward. *Loose bolts on the railing,* he thought. *Falling apart*—he windmilled his arms desperately—*no, just falling*—trying to regain his balance—*too late to bail.* He landed on the cement stairs with jarring impact, banging his hip on the handrail. His board shot out from under him and his lurching momentum carried him forward into the start of the second railing.

He had a split second to notice that the railing's end cap was missing before the jagged metal edge plunged into his stomach.

In the distance, he heard Layla scream.

8

Evan blinked. He wasn't sure if it had been
seconds or minutes since he had fallen.
Seconds, he guessed, his eyes blearily trying to
focus on Layla running toward him.

He was still doubled over the railing. Had
he been impaled? He didn't feel anything. *That
would be the shock*, he could hear Layla's mother
saying in her professional doctor voice. He
gingerly tilted his head down to see how bad
the injury was. The railing seemed to go into
his stomach, but there was no blood, no pain.
Keeping the rest of his body still, he extended
his arm to feel his back. There was a large lump,
but the pipe hadn't gone through. It was as if—

With a strangled yell of surprise, Evan pushed himself back off the railing. It didn't hurt. *Shouldn't it hurt?* It wasn't even sore. He frantically felt his stomach. There was a hole in the sweatshirt fabric, but nothing on his skin, no cuts or marks or bruises . . .

Layla continued to stare at him without saying anything. He hadn't seen pain and fear like that in his best friend since Mr. Hakim had to go to the hospital for a burst appendix.

"I'm all right," wheezed Evan. "I'm all right."

Layla's eyes were wide, and Evan thought he could see her trembling.

"What just happened?" she asked.

Evan shrugged weakly. "I don't know."

"I thought you were—I thought—" Layla's voice shook.

"I don't suppose you recorded that?" Evan asked, trying to distract her.

Layla shook her head numbly. "I—no, I dropped the camera."

Evan found the video camera lying in the grass. He brushed the dirt off and handed it to Layla to check for any damage.

"Hey, you!" Layla shouted suddenly, looking over Evan's shoulder.

Evan turned. At the edge of the park stood one of the middle schoolers who rode their bikes around the neighborhood. The boy startled and took off, and Evan could see the glint of a phone in his hand.

"I'm gonna go ahead and guess that he saw it all," Evan said. "We should get home."

After convincing Layla that he was fine and didn't need her mother to look him over, Evan staggered home to bed. He hadn't been injured—somehow—but he was mentally and physically exhausted. He was too numb to reflect on what had happened. His dad was washing dishes in the kitchen and Isaac was already asleep, so Evan was able to sneak into his own room without anyone looking too closely. Sleep came almost instantly.

***

The next morning, Evan rolled out of bed and out of habit went to go check the website. He blinked sleepily, trying to make sense of the number he was seeing—5,785.

Almost 6,000 hits. And it was climbing even as he looked at it.

The comments seemed to be discussing a video that had been uploaded to someone's blog. He clicked on the link.

It was the phone video from the middle schooler at the skate park. It had to be. The footage was grainier and shakier than it would have been from Layla's camera, but it was clear that it was Stretch Guy in his signature black outfit. Layla couldn't be seen in the video from this angle, thankfully.

Fully aware that he was watching himself, Evan still felt a weird sense of detachment as he saw Stretch Guy stumble and hit the handrail.

But the railing didn't go through him. Instead his back bowed out, like a balloon expanding.

He looked at his stomach again. Even this morning, there were no bruises.

He scrolled through the comments on the video in a daze.

Impenetrable, they said. *Indestructible. Unbreakable.*

Bulletproof.

He dressed quickly and met Layla to walk to school together. Her shock from the night before was gone—instead her face was bright with excitement.

She held up her hand when she saw him. "Before you ask, *no*, we're not going to test and see if you really are bulletproof. I draw the line there."

"I'm not *that* crazy," Evan said with a teasing grin.

Layla raised an eyebrow.

"I have to admit," she said as they walked, "that I lay awake for quite awhile last night worrying that you might have internal bleeding—"

She really is Dr. Hakim's daughter, Evan thought.

"But then I realized that maybe the same thing that makes you stretchy has turned your skin into rubber. Maybe your bones and organs too."

"That would explain why I bounced when I fell—er, leaped off that building."

Layla leaned in closer and poked him in the arm.

"Hey!" Evan said, swatting her hand away. "Stop that."

"Hmm," she said, peering at him and pretending to adjust a pair of glasses like her mother would. "You don't *feel* like a weird rubber mutant."

Evan snorted. "Well, thanks for that."

From the moment they arrived at school, it became clear that all anyone wanted to talk about was Stretch Guy. Even the teachers made only half-hearted attempts to control the whispered conversations in the back of their classes. Evan suspected it was because they were just as eager to hear the rumors. Sophie's story now involved Stretch Guy shielding her from bullets. Mr. Mendez, who had previously been silent about his attempted mugging, insisted that Stretch Guy had saved his life by pulling him out of the way of a moving car.

Evan spent the day giddy with all the attention. Even though it wasn't directed *at* him, it was still *about* him. He walked around with a secret smile, feeling like the fact that he wasn't demanding special treatment for his contributions to society made him even more noble.

9

"You're just loving this, aren't you?"

Leave it to Layla to bring him back to reality.

Evan set down his lunch tray at the table next to her. "As a matter of fact, I am," he said. "I thought for my next video we could make it look like I rescue someone from a burning building."

"I'm not getting involved in arson," Layla said, gesturing with a forkful of potatoes.

"No, we're not actually going to set a building on fire—we'll just do it with special effects."

Layla pursed her lips.

"What? Is it hard to do stuff like that?"

Layla sighed. "I think you'd be a more successful superhero if you spent more time trying to help people and less time trying to make yourself look cooler than you are."

"I haven't been able to *find* any crime!" Evan said.

"Your problem is that you keep thinking about it like everything you do has to have some huge, world-changing impact. Why don't you focus on small things? You managed to save that cat."

"Yeah, I guess, but no one even saw me do that, so what's the point?"

"I thought you wanted to actually make a difference."

"I do, but what's the harm in getting a little recognition for my efforts?"

Layla sighed again. "Okay, fine, we'll work on your next video this weekend."

"Oh," Evan said. "I was kind of thinking it would be tonight."

Layla didn't answer. She didn't even look up from her food.

Evan was about to ask her what was wrong, when Layla took a deep breath and set down her fork.

"I didn't know how to tell you this—"

"Yeah?" Evan prompted.

"—but Sick Trick Industries accepted my application to film the competition tonight."

"*What?*" He had said it so loudly that people at the next table looked over. Evan leaned in and lowered his voice. "What are you talking about?"

"Remember?" Layla asked sarcastically. "They were going to pick a student filmmaker? I had to submit a sample of my work and write an essay? I spent *three weeks* getting my application ready?"

"Of course I remember," Evan hissed. "But you didn't turn them down?"

"Don't give me that," Layla said, glaring at him. "You were the one who encouraged me to apply in the first place."

"Yeah, when I thought that I would make it to the semifinals. What's the point if we're not there together?" He had assumed he would advance to the next round of the competition, side by side with his best friend, cheering each other on. His chest ached when he thought of Layla going without him.

"Oh, and if you can't have your dream, then no one can."

Evan could feel his face grow hot. "No, I just thought—"

"Evan, this is a great opportunity for me. I can put it on my scholarship application."

"And the film about me isn't a great opportunity?"

Layla pressed her lips together and stabbed at her potatoes. Evan could practically hear her grinding her teeth. Finally she said, "The video about Stretch Guy is just a side project. This is a real job. I'll get paid for it."

A small voice in the back of his head told Evan that he was being irrational, but he couldn't help himself. "I would have thought that our friendship meant more to you than money," he said, keeping his eyes on his plate.

He heard a chair scrape loudly and when he looked up, Layla was gone.

"Here's fine," Evan told his dad when they were a couple of blocks away from Greenfair Gardens later that day. "I can walk the rest of the way."

His dad looked unsure, but he pulled up to the curb to let Evan out. Evan had convinced his dad to drive him across town after school so he could watch the Skate Semifinals.

"And you're sure Layla can give you a ride home?" his dad asked.

Evan's stomach squirmed. "Yeah," he lied, "she just had to get over here early, but she'll drop me off after. I'll be home before dark." Layla hadn't said a word to him since lunch and hadn't responded to any of his text apologies.

"Sounds good," his dad said as Evan got out of the car. "Oh, and Evan?"

Evan froze with his hand on the car door. His dad's tone sounded far too casual. "Yeah?"

"You haven't seen my jogging mask, have you?"

Evan gulped. "That dorky thing you wear when you go running in the winter? Last I checked, it was in the hall closet." Either his dad was psychic or the universe had a weird sense of humor.

Evan made sure his mask was secure as he rolled toward the skateboard area of Greenfair. A crowd milled around the entrance to the skate park, spectators chatting and participants adjusting their helmets. A new banner read: SICK TRICK TEEN SKATE SEMIFINALS TODAY!

I should have been here competing, Evan thought. But he didn't have time to be bitter. Because he was going to show them what real skills looked like.

He skated up to the entrance arch where the banner hung. He stretched his arms up and grabbed the top of the arch.

A hush fell as people craned their necks to see what was going on. Evan thought he heard some whispers of recognition.

Evan swung himself up and over the arch. At the top of his movement, he let go and did a somersault in the air. Then he landed on the ground, still on his board, and skated into the park, arms raised over his head in victory.

Cheers erupted from the crowd behind him. Evan was glad the mask covered his mouth because he was grinning like crazy.

Out of the corner of his eye, he thought he could see Layla with her camera near the judges' table, but he ignored her. *If she doesn't have time for me, I don't have time for her.*

Evan had even thought of an exit. He wasn't about to let himself be caught by the crowd. He skated to the chain-link fence that ran around the perimeter of the skate section of the park and did an ollie over it, adding in his 2520-degree spin.

Once safely on the other side, he shouted to the crowd. "If you want to see more sweet moves like that, then meet me on the steps of City Hall in twenty minutes!"

With a jaunty mock salute to the spectators, he slipped away down the hiking trail and into the trees. His plan was to wait a few minutes at the picnic shelter nearby to let the crowd gather at City Hall. Then, he would make his grand entrance to roaring cheers and applause.

Layla was waiting for him when he arrived at the picnic shelter. Evan knew she must have taken the paved road, which was a more direct path than the hiking trail. "What the heck was that?" she demanded.

"Wasn't that cool?" Evan's blood was still pumping with excitement, and for a brief moment he convinced himself that Layla would have forgiven him.

"Cool isn't really the word I was looking for," Layla said.

Evan's smile faded. He hadn't seen her this angry since fourth grade when a kid had made fun of her dad's accent.

"Whoa, what's the matter, Layla? I was just having some fun."

"What's the *matter?*" Layla spluttered. "You ruined my video of the skate tournament. Everyone left to go see you skate at City Hall. They had to reschedule the semifinals."

Evan's plan had worked, but he felt the excitement slipping away from him, leaving him hollow. "Ruined it? If anything, I made it better." He leaned against the picnic table, trying to project confidence he no longer felt. "You said you wouldn't have time to film Stretch Guy, so I figured you could multitask if I combined the two." That was a lie, he realized. His only real goal had been to get back at the judges and show them they'd made a mistake in passing him up.

"That's not your call," Layla shouted. "I was doing all this as a friend. Not because I think it's my 'debt to society' to record every single moment of Stretch Guy's stupid tricks. You haven't even done anything heroic."

"You take that back!" Evan shouted. "I'm going to make a difference!"

Layla gave a sarcastic laugh. "Sure, right after you're done showing off. I should have realized that's all you would care about—looking cool."

She shouldered her camera bag. Somehow her calm coldness was more frightening than her yelling. "You know what I think? You didn't qualify for the semifinals because sometimes you get this whole arrogant, self-important attitude. You're a good skater, Evan, but not great. And instead of practicing to get better, you just complain that people don't recognize your talent."

"Hey," Evan said, putting a hand up. "I tried really hard for that competition. You know that."

"I believe you tried," Layla said, "but you didn't do anything amazing. You didn't take any risks. You didn't try to stand out. You used only the easiest tricks—you stick with what you know because that's what's safe. And now with this new ability, you had a chance to make a difference in our city, but you're just spending your time showing off and *pretending* to be a hero. You always look for the easy way. I could deal with it with the skating, but I'm tired of waiting around for you to finally do some real good with your power. You're walking around like you're this town's greatest gift, but from what I've seen, you've done nothing."

She turned on her heel and stormed off down the paved road that led to the parking lot.

Late afternoon sunlight dappled the cement at the edge of the picnic shelter. Evan hadn't really given any thought to how he would get home. He had been hoping, he admitted to himself, that he and Layla would make up and she'd give him a ride. They bickered all the time, but this was the first serious fight they had had. *What if she never forgives me?*

Evan pushed the terrible thought out of his head and made his way to the edge of the park. There was no sign of Layla's yellow jeep. He thought about taking the city bus home, but he didn't have any money for the bus fare. He sighed and started skating home, stretch-propelling himself whenever he was sure no one was watching. He didn't hurry—he didn't want to have to explain to his dad why he was home so early and without Layla.

He was halfway there when his phone started to blow up with notifications. He sat down on a nearby bus stop bench and pulled out his phone. Soon he was absorbed in watching the counter go up on his website. After the railing-accident video, Layla had changed the website permissions so that other people could post videos. People were now uploading phone footage of Stretch Guy's appearance at the skate tournament. It looked even cooler than Evan had hoped.

But then he started to see comments like *It's okay, Stretch Guy will save them,* and *Stretch Guy, where are you?* He heard a low droning sound and looked up to see a news helicopter fly overhead. He went to a local news site to see what was up. They had the breaking news streaming: there had been a serious car accident over on the new freeway interchange. It seemed a semi had crashed and there was a huge pileup—and the wreckage was keeping emergency responders from getting to everyone in time. That explained the comments on social media. They all wanted Stretch Guy to come save people.

Evan felt his stomach curl up in knots. He had never actually faced danger like that before. How would his stretch powers even be useful in an emergency like this? What if he got hurt—or even *died?* It was probably better if he stayed out of the way and let the professionals take care of everything. Besides, with his secret identity, no one could ever blame Evan Wu-Kopecky if Stretch Guy didn't show up. No one ever had to know.

He opened a game app to distract himself, trying to ignore the constant buzz and flash of notifications. He thought he could hear the wail of sirens in the distance, but maybe that was his imagination, fed by the guilt he felt every time he saw a new comment pop up.

His phone rang. Evan put it on speakerphone so he could continue his game.

"Hi, Dr. Hakim, what's up?"

"Have you seen Layla?" her mother asked.

There was something in her voice that made Evan feel cold with fear. He exited out of his game. "She drove home after the skate tournament." He left out the fight they had. He checked the time. "But that was almost an hour ago."

"I'm at work and my colleagues in the ER say that they're getting a bunch of patients in from a major car crash. Layla was supposed to meet me at the hospital after her film project so we could go out for dinner. She hasn't shown up and she's not answering her phone. Do you think she's all right? Have you heard from her since the tournament?"

Evan switched to his newsfeed and saw something that nearly made his heart stop. There was video footage from a news helicopter flying over the scene of the accident. Evan recognized it as the freeway interchange near Greenfair Gardens. That was when he noticed the yellow jeep in the middle of the rubble, its front crumpled.

Evan felt panic constricting his throat.

He could try to convince himself that there had to be other yellow jeeps in the world.

But there was no use denying it.

Deep in his gut he knew it was Layla's jeep.

10

"Evan? Are you still there?"

"I'm gonna have to call you back, Dr. Hakim. But don't worry, I'll let you know the instant I know something."

"Wait, what—"

Evan nearly dropped his cell phone as he hung up. He threw his skateboard down and hopped on, taking off back the way he had come, toward Greenfair Gardens and the freeway interchange.

At least he was already in his Stretch Guy costume. He tried to ignore the suffocating feeling of the jogging mask. He moved sluggishly like he was dreaming. He willed his limbs, clumsy with fear, to move faster. As he sped down the street, he briefly wondered if he should do some stretches before something like this, like an athlete would. Stretch Guy stretching. He knew Layla would have laughed at that.

His heart thudded against his rib cage as he got closer. *Please be all right.* She had to be all right. The last conversation they had had been angry. He had to apologize for being such a self-centered show-off.

He had to save her.

Next to the freeway, there was a frontage road that was rarely busy. Evan pumped his leg as fast as he could as he made his way down the road. When he could see the pileup in the distance, Evan stretched his legs easily to scale the fence between the road and the freeway. He approached the scene of the accident, feeling ill-prepared. He had hoped the ride over would make things clearer for him, but he still had no idea how to help.

The air was filled with a commotion of shouts and sirens. Emergency workers ran back and forth at the ground level, giving directions in clear, loud voices that sounded much calmer than Evan felt. News helicopters whirred overhead, while police officers shepherded concerned bystanders out of the way. No one seemed to have noticed Evan yet.

He looked up to where the interchange arched above him, swooping along on five different overpasses. He could see the signs of the pileup from down here. A huge semi-truck had crashed into the barrier and was dangling with almost half of its front edge off the bridge above him. It was blocking any emergency vehicles that tried to approach from the other side of the wreckage.

Evan had seen from the helicopter footage that emergency vehicles had gotten as close as they could both up on the overpass and down here at street level. Police had blocked off the scene, forcing any additional traffic off the freeway before it got close. Emergency medical responders had set up triage stations at street level. He knew from Dr. Hakim's stories that these were for treating people with light injuries and for stabilizing people with serious injuries so the ambulances could rush them to the hospital. The emergency workers were doing their best, but an accident of this scale was challenging.

Evan couldn't see Layla's jeep from here.

"Hey, kid!" an EMT shouted as Evan ran past. "You can't go near there! It's too dangerous!"

Evan skidded to a halt. "But—" He couldn't think of a reasonable explanation other than the obvious. "I'm Stretch Guy."

"Who?" asked the EMT, looking confused and annoyed. "Look, I don't care who you are, you need to get out of here—"

A girl was standing a few feet away, recording everything on her phone. "Ohmygod! Stretch Guy!"

Evan didn't recognize her, but it wasn't really surprising to him anymore that random people knew of Stretch Guy.

"I knew you would come!" she said. "It's all right," she told the EMT, "Stretch Guy is here to help."

The EMT frowned. "Who is Stretch Guy—?"

But Evan had already run past. As if in answer to the EMT's question, he stretched his arms up over his head and grabbed the edge of the freeway overpass. He yanked his arms back with all his might and he flew up into the air like a slingshot. He thought he heard the girl whoop behind him. He popped up over the edge of the overpass, and then tumbled down. Years of skateboarding had taught him how to fall properly, and he caught the impact by rolling on his shoulder.

He pushed himself up and scanned the area for any sign of Layla's yellow jeep. EMTs moved from car to car in small groups, efficiently dealing with each victim's situation. Evan could see more flashing lights, but they were on the other side of the pileup, with wrecked and burning cars blocking the way.

It was starting to get dark, and the setting sun burned blood red through the smog. He coughed, thinking again how stupid their fight had been, how Layla had been right all along.

When Evan spotted the totaled yellow jeep, he sprinted toward it. The jeep must have hit the car in front of it. The hood was smashed and twisted, and a spiderweb of cracks filled the windshield, but otherwise the damage to the jeep wasn't too bad. Pop music still blared from the stereo.

"Layla?" He peered into the jeep, trying to see if his friend was okay. He saw her lying motionless in the driver's seat and for a heart stopping moment he couldn't tell if she was breathing or not. But then she moaned with pain and her eyes opened to look at him. They opened wider.

"Evan? Is that you?" Layla tried to move and winced. "What happened?" Her eyes focused on the scene outside her window. "Oh my god."

"Are you all right? You're not badly hurt, are you?" Evan asked.

Layla frowned. "I don't think so." She reached forward and put the jeep in park, biting back a yell as she turned off the ignition. "Okay, never mind, my chest is killing me.

Cracked ribs, I guess? I don't know. At least I can move my arms and feet. So I'm not paralyzed."

"I'm going to get you out of here," Evan said.

He yanked open her car door, then paused. Evan had no idea how to get her out of the car without hurting her more. Layla saw his hesitation and reached a hand out to him. They braced their arms against one another so they were relatively bracketed and secure. Then Evan gingerly pulled Layla from her seat.

She yelped as she stood up. "Ugh, I think my ankle is busted too. Or at least twisted."

Letting Layla lean heavily on his shoulder, Evan hobbled to the side of the overpass.

"There are emergency triage stations down there that can get you patched up," he told her. "It'll be safer anyway."

"How are you going to get me down?" Layla asked, looking at the drop, which was at least thirty feet.

Evan hadn't thought this far ahead. "Umm, I guess I'll stretch you down."

Layla looked unsure as Evan wrapped his arms around her, coiling them so that they supported her back and didn't squeeze her injured ribs. "Look," he told her, "it's either this or I stretch into a giant slide and I don't know if anyone wants to see that."

Layla managed a little laugh but then stiffened in pain.

Cradling his friend in his arms, Evan stood on his left leg and stuck his right leg over the edge of the railing. He stretched his right leg down until it hit the ground below. Then he shifted his weight to stand on his right foot and swung his left leg over the railing, followed by the right. Now that he was standing on the ground below, he shortened his legs, and he and Layla descended like an elevator as he lowered to his normal height.

Evan set Layla down gently near an emergency responder, who was staring at him, mouth open in amazement.

Evan shrugged.

The emergency responder shook her head and refocused on Layla. As she bent to

examine her newest patient, Evan realized
that Layla's parents didn't know their daughter
was safe. He sent a quick text message to let
Dr. Hakim know and promised her details. A
moment later he heard a couple of emergency
responders nearby shouting and pointing up at
the overpass.

"The cars near the tanker truck are leaking
fuel, and the flames are spreading," the first
EMT said.

"Isn't that tanker truck full of hazardous
materials?" the second EMT asked, eyes wide.

"Yeah, they think it could explode at any
moment. We need to get as many people out
of there as we can," the first EMT instructed,
and the second EMT ran off to spread the
message.

Evan's stomach churned when he thought
of all the cars up there. "Wait here," he told
Layla. "I'm going back in."

"Really?" Layla asked. "But you heard
them. It's dangerous!"

Evan took a deep breath, steeling
himself. "You were right. It's time for me

to do something truly heroic." He grinned mischievously. "And prove there's more to me than good looks and cool moves."

He turned away quickly so he wouldn't have to think too hard about the fear in her eyes.

He used the slingshot move to get back up to the crash. In the back of his mind he wondered what he was doing this for. He didn't know these people.

But he might be the only person who had a chance to save them all in time. He had to do *something*.

At the first car he approached, the passenger was trying to free the unconscious driver, but the windshield had shattered, and broken glass littered the ground around the car.

The passenger took off his coat and wrapped it around his hand and lower arm.

"What are you doing?" Evan panted as he ran over.

The passenger hardly spared Evan a glance. "Gotta protect my arm before I reach through the window."

Jagged glass framed the broken car window.

"Here, let me," Evan said, pushing up his sweatshirt sleeve.

"Whoa, dude, what are you—"

The passenger fell silent as Evan stretched his arm through the window. Glass scraped over his arm but didn't break the skin. He reached over the unconscious driver and undid the seatbelt, then tried to pull the door handle from the inside. It jiggled but the handle didn't seem to connect to the door. It was just a bit of plastic.

"Handle on that door's always been a piece of junk," the passenger stammered. "Sometimes—sometimes Jamal has to use the other door and crawl over to—" he trailed off, gesturing vaguely at the passenger side door. "But it's locked."

Evan realized what the passenger had been trying to accomplish. Evan leaned in close so he could see the buttons on the inside of the door. He hastily pressed the unlock button. The car clicked, and the passenger ran around to open the door.

Evan saw an EMT approach the car and, figuring that they knew best how to get the driver out and treat him medically, he moved on to continue searching for more people to help.

He thought he heard the passenger yell thank you after him, but it was hard to tell over the sound of the alarm blaring from an abandoned and entirely wrecked station wagon next to him.

Evan made his way along the road, helping where he could, snaking his arm through tight spaces the EMTs couldn't reach and past scalding metal pipes without injury. Some of the people he helped were able to make their way to the emergency responders once Evan had freed them from the wreckage. Some had bad injuries that made it impossible for them to walk, and in those cases Evan cleared the way so the emergency responders could get them strapped to stretchers and safely carried away. At one point, Evan stood between the responders and a burning car as a shield, stretching himself wider so that they could tend to a victim without having to worry about the flames.

A few minutes later, someone started yelling.

Evan looked around and realized that the flames had reached the tanker truck.

"Get out of here!" an emergency responder shouted to anyone within earshot. "It's going to blow! Get out of here *now*."

Evan could see there were still more people trapped in their cars.

And even those who were free and were running away from the truck as fast as they could, supported and helped along by emergency responders, were never going to make it in time.

He stood frozen for a split second, staring at the hazardous chemicals sign on the side of the truck until it seemed to fill his vision. He thought of the explosion ripping everything apart. He thought of the toxic chemicals that would rain down on everyone.

Evan bounded forward, stepping over the smoking masses of twisted metal and other obstacles with his abnormally long and springy legs.

Part of his brain told him he was being ridiculous. That was the part that enjoyed watching the visitor counter on his website climb higher.

But part of him, the part of him that had jumped into action when he had seen that Layla was alive, or even when he had rescued that stupid cat—that part urged him forward. There would be no glory.

But it was the right thing to do.

He figured he only had seconds to make a decision. He thought about trying to dampen the fire and put it out, but he knew somehow that it was too late for that.

He stretched himself out, flatter and flatter like a pancake, until he formed a protective bubble around the entire truck.

And he wasn't a moment too soon. There was a creaking, wrenching sound, and even though it didn't burn his skin, Evan could still feel the searing heat and energy unfolding underneath him. Suddenly there was a muffled *whump* from the explosion. He held his form another moment, waiting to see if anything else would happen, before finally deciding it was okay to step back.

Before he could though, Evan felt the world begin to spin. *Just hold on*, he told himself. *Get back to your normal size before anyone finds you.*

He could feel the edges of his vision closing in. He was going to pass out. As his body shrunk back to its normal size, Evan's eyes briefly rolled up toward the sky. And then everything went dark.

11

When Evan awoke in the hospital, Layla was the first person he saw.

"What happened?" Evan croaked, his throat sore from breathing in smoke.

"Hey," Layla said with a soft smile. She was sitting in the chair next to him, bandages wound around her cracked ribs and a few stitches on her face. She had a brace on her foot and ankle, and Evan saw a set of crutches leaning against the wall. But Layla was alive. And that was all that mattered at that moment. "You did it. You saved everyone from the explosion."

"Oh." He wished he had something more dramatic, more meaningful to say in such a moment. Instead, his eyes drifted around the room.

"Don't worry, your dad and Isaac are with my mom outside." Layla gestured to the closed door behind her.

"How long have I been here?" he asked, pushing himself up in the bed.

Layla blinked at the question and glanced at the wall clock. "Umm, a few hours. It's not even midnight."

Evan frowned. "I'm exhausted, but I feel fine otherwise. Why am I here?"

"Oh, you're not injured. My mom just wanted them to triple check." Layla leaned in close. "She freaked out a little when she couldn't insert the IV—the needle wouldn't pierce your skin—but I explained everything to her. She's insisted that she be the only one to treat you now." Layla winked theatrically. "So your secret is safe."

"I'm just glad *you're* safe." Evan felt happy tears prick at his eyes.

Layla smiled. "Thanks again for coming to get me. I can't believe you threw yourself over an exploding truck. I freaked out when I smelled burning rubber, but it turned out it was just car tires."

Evan laughed.

"You should see the Stretch Guy website," Layla said. "The crash was so bad it was on national news, and between helicopter footage and bystanders with phones, there's a bunch of videos of you doing the whole superhero thing. The visitor counter just went past one *million* and it keeps climbing."

Evan was surprised to find that the number didn't thrill him like it used to. "You know what?"

"What?" Layla asked.

"My manager really deserves a break."

"I agree," Layla said, smirking.

Evan searched for the remote. When he couldn't find it, he stretched his arm across the room to turn the TV on.

He flopped back against the pillows with a contented sigh. "I think Stretch Guy is going to go on vacation for a while." He winked at Layla. "At least until after the next chemistry exam."

ONE YEAR LATER

LOCAL TEEN HERO CONTINUES TO STRETCH EXPECTATIONS

Stretch Guy is the new spokesperson for Sick Trick Industries. The stretchy crusader, who saved many lives in the freeway accident last year, has millions of followers on social media. But he insists that he's not in it for the free skateboard gear. "I'm just trying to do what's right, trying to make a difference in the community and in the lives of the people I care about." He teaches youth skateboarding classes for free, on top of his full-time job as a superhero.

In related news, local girl Layla Hakim, director of *Stretched Too Thin*, the full-length documentary of Stretch Guy's rise to fame, is up for a Teen Filmmaker of the Year award.

HAVING A SUPERPOWER IS NOT AS EASY
AS THE COMIC BOOKS MAKE IT SEEM.

CHECK OUT ALL OF THE TITLES IN THE

SUPER HUMAN

SERIES

MIND OVER MATTER

NOW YOU SEE ME

PICKING UP SPEED

STRETCHED TOO THIN

STRONGHOLD

TAKE TO THE SKIES

WHAT WOULD YOU DO IF YOU WOKE UP IN A
VIDEO GAME?

CHECK OUT ALL OF THE TITLES IN THE

LEVEL UP

SERIES

[ALIEN INVASION] [LABYRINTH] [POD RACER]
[REALM OF MYSTICS] [SAFE ZONE]
[THE ZEPHYR CONSPIRACY]

DAY OF DISASTER

AFTERSHOCK
BACKFIRE
BLACK BLIZZARD
DEEP FREEZE
VORTEX
WALL OF WATER

Would you survive?

ABOUT THE AUTHOR

Raelyn Drake lives in Minneapolis, Minnesota with her husband and rescue corgi mix, Sheriff, who refuses to learn how to skateboard (even though he would be really good at it).